MINDFUL

MR. SLOTH

KATY HUDSON

CAPSTONE EDITIONS
a capstone imprint

Published by Capstone Editions,
an imprint of Capstone
1710 Roe Crest Drive
North Mankato, Minnesota 56003
capstonepub.com

Library of Congress Cataloging-in-Publication
Data is available on the Library of Congress
website.

ISBN: 9781684468249 (paperback)

Designer: Kay Fraser

Printed and bound in China. PO 5067

Summary: Sasha loves
to do lots of things, all at
once, as fast as possible.
Mr. Sloth loves to do
things one at a time, at a
nice, easy pace. Can Mr.
Sloth's mindful ways teach
Sasha to slow down and
enjoy each moment?

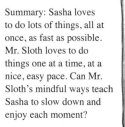

Sasha Patience Pruitt was far from patient.

She loved to do lots of things, all at once.

She had one speed—fast.

Early one morning, Sasha raced up to her tree house, trampling some flowers along the way. She frantically waved her butterfly net around for two seconds and moved on.

She had just whipped out her guitar to serenade the birds when she was interrupted by an almighty CRASH above her head.

Sasha scrambled up
to the roof to find . . .

. . . a sloth.

"Heeeellllloooo," he said.
"My name . . . is . . . Mrrrr . . .
Slooooo . . ."

Mr. Sloth was going to
explain how he had fallen
from the branch above
during his morning nap,
but Sasha was too impatient
to wait for his story.

"Come along, Mr. Sloth," she said. "We are going to be best friends. I have so much for us to do together!"

They tried playing doctor, but Mr. Sloth took far too long to find a heartbeat.

Sasha decided that Mr. Sloth should be the patient. That worked better.

They tried building a rocket, but Mr. Sloth was much too slow with the sticky tape.

Sasha thought it best that he do a different job.

Painting took even longer! Sasha had painted
FOUR pictures in the time it took Mr. Sloth
to tie his apron.

"Come along now,"
Sasha said, picking
up a paintbrush and
taking over. "There!
All done!"

"Grab a helmet, Mr. Sloth! It's time for the neighborhood race!"

Off Sasha and Mr. Sloth sped, faster than anyone else in the race. Faster and faster they went, until . . .

"Stoooooop," howled Mr. Sloth.

"What is it?" Sasha asked impatiently.

"Caaan you hear . . . that biiirrrrd . . . singing?" he asked. "Beeeeaaaauuttiful."

Sasha paused. The chirping was nice enough, but she had a race to win. She plopped Mr. Sloth back in her bike basket.

Off they sped again, Sasha pedaling
fast to catch up until . . .

"Stoooooop," moaned Mr. Sloth.

With a quick huff, Sasha stopped.
"What is it now, Mr. Sloth?"

"Caaan . . . you . . . smeeellll the . . . flowwwwwerrrrs?" he asked. "Mmmm."

Sasha sniffed around, pausing a little longer this time. The flowers did smell nice. How had she never noticed that before?

But she didn't have time for this—the race was still underway.

"Helmet back on, Mr. Sloth," she said. "Let's go!"

Off they raced once more, Sasha pedaling as fast as she could, until . . .

"Stoooop," wheezed
Mr. Sloth.

Once again, Sasha
slammed on the brakes.

But before she could ask, Mr. Sloth took off
his helmet and whispered, "Shhhhh . . ."

Sasha waited. She took a breath. She felt a
tiny breeze. She looked. She listened.

All was still.

That day Sasha saw that fun had two speeds—
fast AND slow. She still liked to go as fast
as she could at times,

but other times,
going slow worked
out much better.

And just like Sasha had predicted, she and
Mr. Sloth became the very best of friends.
At the end of every day, they would snuggle
together for story time.

Mr. Sloth took so long to read the words that
Sasha got to enjoy every part of the story
more than she ever had before. She even had
time to look at the pictures!

Of course, they didn't always
make it to the end . . .

MINDFULNESS is being present in the moment.

FOCUS on where you are and what you are doing.

STOP. RELAX.

THINK about your breathing.

USE YOUR SENSES to notice the world around you.